Killer, Killer, Lobster & Chicken Dinner

A Newfound Lake Cozy Mystery
Book 15

Virginia K. Bennett

To the members of the writing community who supported me early on, thank you!

Skye Jones
Marissa Farrar
Dawn Edwards
Kat Reads Romance
Kathryn LeBlanc
TL Swan
VR Tennent
Gina Sturino
Rachelle Kampen
...and so many more!

Table of Contents

Chapter 1

The Schedule

Rebecca looked across the kitchen island at Kenny. "It's been officially open for a few weeks now, so how do you like the new building?"

"It's a dream come true." He continued to eat the mushroom and cheese omelet Rebecca had cooked along with a side of potatoes she fried up in a pan.

The police station and fire department in Bristol were both in dire need of replacement, and the town took forever to pass the needed budget to produce a new building combining all of the emergency services for the town. Kenny had been the police chief throughout the whole process and was proud to have seen it come to fruition. The joining of the two departments, including ambulance services, would lead to fewer communication issues and more collaborative training.

"It's especially helpful for the new fire chief to be right next door, learning the ropes and all."

With the loss of the long-time fire chief at the start of

the summer, Kenny would be working closely with Roger Vatra, the former fire chief of a small town in Vermont. While his knowledge of working with firefighters in the department would come in handy – much like a teacher having good classroom management skills – his ability to work for a tourist town like Bristol would have some growing pains. A wife and two small children had moved to Bristol along with Chief Vatra.

"What do you think of the new fire chief?" Rebecca helped herself to a forkful of fluffy scrambled eggs followed by a bite of crispy bacon. Using this method, she didn't need to salt her eggs.

"He has a great demeanor with the members of his department, and we'll catch him up on the inner workings of the area quickly. Maybe we could invite his family over to dinner."

"I'd love that. Want to have them come here for dinner?"

Kenny smiled and took Rebecca's hand across the island. "I don't want to assume that you will host a dinner for my co-workers. I'm happy to do all, most or some of the work. Whatever makes the most sense." He kissed the top of her hand.

"Well, we'll have four children, right?"

"That's true." Kenny shook his head side to side. "I almost forget what it's like to entertain them so small."

"I'm happy to cook the dinner if you can help manage the children with Chief Vatra and his wife."

"I'll buy everything, just give me a list."

"You're not getting out of it that easy." She let go of

his hand and walked around the island, wrapping her arms around his waist. "You need to find out what they like and if we need to make anything special for the kids. Consider that your first assignment."

He gave her a partial salute. "Yes, ma'am. Orders received."

They laughed together. "Now, let's finish breakfast and get ready for a long day."

The day ahead of them was, no question, one of the busiest days on the calendar for the town of Bristol and the Newfound Lake area. First, they needed to show up at the pancake breakfast hosted by the Masonic Union Lodge, though they didn't plan on eating again. Rebecca knew at this age she'd end up looking too much like a hobbit if she ate second breakfast. After that, there was an antique car show Kenny wanted to check out before Rebecca got time to peruse the stalls and stands for local vendors, food, games and music.

Bristol Old Home Day was an event everyone looked forward to, especially children. Heather, Kenny's ex-wife, would join them with their daughters, Melanie and Megan, after the car show for a few hours in Kelley Park. It was mostly the playground, games and food that enticed them to participate, but the Fire vs. Police softball game was the climax for the blended family.

"Are the girls excited to watch the game?" Rebecca asked Kenny as they got ready to leave.

"They enjoy the first couple innings, but they'll skip out on the end to get in line for the Lobster & Chicken Dinner."

"Can I join them?" Rebecca smirked.

"You don't want to be there to support the police station? You know, that's practically written into the wedding vows."

She nodded. "I'll be there, and we can get dinner when you're done, provided you aren't too stinky."

"Oh, I'll be stinky, alright, but I'll bring a change of clothes to help."

They went to climb into his SUV, but Rebecca stopped. "Why don't I at least get my car to the library. If anything should happen, I can always walk back from Kelley Park and not need to bother you."

"Are you trying to jinx us?"

"I'd never do that, but you know what they say, an ounce of prevention is worth a pound of cure. Meet you at the library."

She got out with her bag of items she might need – sunscreen, water bottle, umbrella and granola bar – and got into her vintage Subaru, turning the key in the ignition.

"New car, new house, new husband, new kids, new, new, new. Life sure is changing in my old age," she said to her mid-forties self as she pulled out of the driveway. She had started the new habit of backing into her driveway as a result of Kenny's propensity to do the same because of his law enforcement background. She also found it to be preferable, in general, to not back out, even when not needing to flee the scene of a crime or get somewhere quickly.

It was convenient that the Masonic Union Lodge

was next door to the library, where they needed to show their faces, at least, in support of the fundraiser. Rebecca got to chat with Mary, her long-time assistant at the library, and wave at a few familiar faces before Kenny tapped her on the shoulder to let her know they could leave.

She joined Kenny in the SUV, leaving her car parked in her usual spot. They took a right out of the library parking lot then turned onto North Main Street, hoping to find a place to park along the one-way street. With no luck, they continued to the parking lot of the middle school and easily found a spot there. They walked, hand in hand, to the opposite end of the field for Kenny to check out the car show.

"Jacob, I didn't know you had a Studebaker." Kenny's jaw gaped open, looking up and down, left to right at the antique. "Where did you come up with the money for this?"

"It was my Pop's car. He left it to me, and I've been fixing it up."

Rebecca waved and continued walking, checking out the other cars on display. She knew nothing about cars in general and certainly not antique ones. Occasionally she stopped to look inside the car if the leather was particularly interesting or the car seemed rare, but it was all superficial. When she made it back around, Kenny was still talking to Jacob.

"So, with you at third and me catching, no one is stealing home."

"Huh, I pegged you as a pitcher," she said to Kenny.

Jacob looked stunned. "How has this never come up?"

"I didn't watch the game last summer, he's not in a league... why would I know?"

"Good point. How's the wedding planning coming?" Jacob figured out too late that he shouldn't have asked the question. Kenny's face paled, and Rebecca looked down at her feet.

"We still haven't nailed down a date, and The Ledge is only open so late in the year, so I guess we need to really make some decisions soon."

"Jacob, what you'll come to realize is that a wedding is so important," he spoke to Rebecca more than Jacob, "that the person you love can take all the time they need to make it perfect."

"Truer words were never spoken." Heather came up behind the trio with the girls in tow. "Kenny is a wonderful man to listen to when it comes to being a good partner."

Rebecca smiled at Heather. She knew it was rare, and she appreciated it, but she was still flabbergasted on a regular basis that neither woman was jealous of the other.

"Dad, we're ready to have fun." Melanie pulled on Kenny's arm.

"Dad, I want to start on the playground, pleeeeeeeeeeease." Megan dragged out the word please for at least five seconds.

"Playground first, then some games. Jacob, see you on the field."

Heather hooked her arm around Rebecca's elbow. "And what can we go look at?"

"Arts and crafts first, or food?"

"Food. I'm starving. See you later, Chief Towne." Heather smiled and did a little finger wave at Kenny as he was forcibly moved in the direction of the playground by his daughters.

"So, I heard what Jacob asked. What's going on with the wedding plans?"

"I'm sure the deck of The Ledge would be nice, but it's just not perfect. I think it's what Kenny wants, though." The two women stopped at the first booth to look at some gorgeous jewelry made by a local retired teacher.

"Kenny wants what you want. He's a good man like that. If you want more time, he'll give you that too." Heather held up a necklace to Rebecca's neck. "That would look nice on you."

Rebecca looked in the small mirror provided by the seller. The color of the beads looked nice against her red hair. "We'll come back to it later."

They walked off, checking out another booth with knitted and crocheted items before finding a place to get fried dough. It's not like fried dough counted as lunch, but the kids weren't there to question the decision, and they'd have a real dinner later.

The day passed easily as they crossed paths with Kenny, Melanie and Megan, with any of the three adults traveling off independently as wanted or needed. Each adult had a wide circle of friends and people they knew from work, so there was no rhyme or reason to who they would run into next.

"It's time for me to get ready for the game. Want to come over when it starts or now?"

The girls both sang out, "Later."

"I guess we'll be there later. Let's go back to the playground." Heather escorted them in the opposite direction of the field, leaving Rebecca to decide where she would go next.

"It's your choice. I'm going to get changed and warm up. Not very exciting, but also much quieter." He smiled in the direction of his girls, though he could have meant Heather as well.

"I'll come with you, before you smell." She pinched her crinkled-up nose.

They walked in the direction of the softball field, near the middle school and the school's bus parking lot. He grabbed his bag from the back of the SUV and changed in the back seat where the windows were tinted. Emerging from the back in a blue uniform, Rebecca was able to appreciate what amazing shape he was in, especially for a man in his mid-forties.

"Looking good, Towne," she cat-called. "I'll have to keep the women off with a stick."

"Just point them in Jacob's direction."

She raised an eyebrow. "I'm not sure the women attracted to you would be the same women he'd be interested in, but we'll see."

She sat on the hillside with her back to the street, remembering how this whole field was taken up by the

Fireman's Carnival about three months earlier. Where that event marked the start of the summer, this marked the end. Melanie and Megan would be going back to school soon, and she'd be into a fall schedule in no time, planning activities for children not yet in school and things to keep the older ones busy after school.

"Here we go police!" she shouted as the two teams took the field.

Kenny looked at her as he walked over to crouch behind the plate. She was close enough for him to say, "We're not up to bat first."

She could feel her cheeks heat with embarrassment.

In no time, the pitcher was warmed up, and Heather joined her on the small hillside with Melanie and Megan.

"Let's go, Dad!" Melanie yelled, loud enough for the right fielder to hear.

"Yeah, Dad," the batter parroted. "Let's go back to when you were about twenty years younger and could throw fast enough to be the pitcher."

"I wouldn't go there if I were you." Kenny motioned to the pitcher, sending him a signal for what pitch to throw. Three strikes later, and the talkative firefighter was silent on the way back to the bench. "Don't worry, I'll make sure you get a chance to run some other time."

Chapter 2

The Dinner

With the game coming to an end in the middle of the ninth, police seven and firefighters five, Kenny was in good spirits, especially after having remembered to talk to Chief Vatra about dinner with his family. He changed, as promised, and joined Rebecca on the short walk to the Lobster & Chicken Dinner.

"Did you already buy tickets?" she asked as they made their way to the other end of the field.

"I bought myself one for chicken and one for lobster. I knew after the game I'd be starving. I bought you one for lobster, but I'll share my chicken with you if you're still hungry."

"Lobster should be fine with me. I think there are also side dishes."

He smiled down at her. "I'm still willing to share... my chicken."

When they arrived at the large tents housing the dinner, they spotted Heather sitting with Melanie and

Megan at a picnic table. Waving at the trio, Rebecca and Kenny got in line for their meals.

The sturdy paper plates were at the start of the line where a volunteer was replenishing supplies as needed. "Got everything? Napkins, utensils?"

"I think we're all set," responded Kenny.

They handed over their tickets to the volunteer before looking up. The lobster went on Kenny's plate first, followed by one on Rebecca's.

"Fancy seeing you here, Jeremy," said Rebecca, surprised to see him.

"Pretty sure we're all on the 'call in case of emergency list' for the Town of Bristol. Morey Bornne called this morning in a panic."

Jeremy was the other regular volunteer at the library along with Mary. As a retired teacher, he knew most of the year-long residents in town because he had been their teacher or grew up with the parents. His commitment to the town and Newfound Lake area was right up there with the best of them.

"Wonder why I didn't get a call," Rebecca mused.

"Probably because she knew you were the head cheerleader at the softball game. And because I told her you'd be busy. I think you were on the list right after me."

"Well, thank you for that."

"I got roped in this morning as well." The man next to Jeremy was no stranger to working town-sponsored events.

"Mr. Bornne, what kind of emergency could have

11

warranted taking away a free night from you?" Rebecca was sarcastic but serious at the same time.

"One butter or two?" he asked.

Barry Bornne ladled melted butter into small plastic containers from a crockpot adjacent to the trays where he had acquired the lobsters. Matching Rebecca's height, he was on the shorter side of average for a man approaching seventy. Both he and Jeremy were often called in at the last minute to help on Morey's projects.

"We'll each take two, please," answered Kenny.

"How'd the game go, Chief?" Barry asked as he handed them the requested butters.

"Police won again. Third year in a row. Just trying to live up to your legacy."

"You'll need another seven wins to match me in my prime," crowed Barry. As a former police officer himself, Barry had been the best hitter for the team back in his day, as he had reminded Kenny several times over the past year or so in Rebecca's presence. It was clear he was reliving his favorite memory every time he spoke of winning the game one year with a walk-off home run.

"We're holding up the line, but I'd love to talk softball when you're off duty."

"I'm married to Morey. I'm never off duty."

"Understood." Kenny and Rebecca continued through the line, collecting Kenny's second dinner of chicken as well as corn, potato salad, drinks and a dessert of strawberry shortcake from a different tent. Kenny got two of each because of the two dinners. "We'll never eat all of this."

"The girls will help, I'm sure."

They approached the table where Heather, Megan and Melanie were seated.

"We're just getting ready to head home, but we wanted to save the table for you two," Heather said as she stood, offering Rebecca her seat. "Girls, want to tell Dad and Rebecca what you did today?"

"We climbed the rock wall."

"We had cotton candy."

"I had blue, Megan had pink."

"I got to sit in a super cool blue car."

"I ate a whole lobster."

"Woah, woah, woah. You ate a whole lobster?" He focused on Melanie.

"I did, and my corn, and my baked potato." Melanie puffed out her chest.

"Guess that's the end of the kids hot dog meal. This day just got a lot more expensive."

Heather rolled her eyes. You don't know the half of it. Next year, the two of you are doing all the morning stuff with the girls, and I'll handle dinner."

Kenny pulled his wallet out. "How much do you want to cover..."

"Don't you bother. We both know it all comes around. Some days you take them to Canobie Lake Park, and other days I just take them to Wellington. It all evens out in the end."

Replacing his wallet, he said, "I'm sure it does. But I don't ever want my job or softball to make things unfair."

"I'll give you a call when they start asking for cars and tuition payments. Let's go girls."

Kenny gave Melanie and Megan hugs before taking a seat recently vacated by them. "I'll see you again tomorrow."

"Let's hope so. I have a date Sunday night."

Rebecca asked, "Do we know him?"

"I don't think so, but you will if he's worth it. I'm not sure most men could handle the five of us, but I'm still looking." She winked and walked off with the girls.

"I never thought about it that way," said Rebecca.

"What way?" Kenny said around a bite of chicken off the bone. He had already managed a mouthful of corn from the cob, and it looked like he'd tried the potato salad as well.

"Anyone that wants to date Heather is taking on not just Heather, but an additional four people. He has to be confident and strong enough to not be intimidated by us as well as the girls."

He appeared to ponder this revelation while he enjoyed his first bite of lobster-claw meat. "Good thing they crack and cut these for us."

"I was set free. Morey relieved me of my lobster duties." Barry joined Rebecca and Kenny at their picnic table. "Let's talk about your game today."

Rebecca smiled at Kenny, knowing he was deciding between two discussions he was equally disinterested in.

"I'd love to tell you about the game," he said with a grin. Kenny proceeded to talk more than eat, but he made sure not to let the lobster or the butter get too cold. Barry asked the occasional question, but mostly focused on his lobster while Kenny gave him the play by play.

Mid-sentence, Barry excused himself to find a bathroom.

"That was odd," Kenny observed before putting another forkful of potato salad into his mouth.

"Rude even, unless he was waiting a long time, but you gave him plenty of opportunities to excuse himself if needed."

With confusion painted over both of their faces, they finished their meals. Kenny had slowed down considerably, but Rebecca easily finished her dinner and was picking at the second side dishes Kenny got with the chicken.

"I know I've said it one hundred times, but side dishes are my favorite."

As she finished that sentence, Morey Bornne came running down the hill from the Community Center. She was yelling something, but it couldn't quite be made out until she got closer. "Barry collapsed! Someone help! Barry collapsed!"

Both Rebecca and Kenny got up and ran to her, following her up to the Community Center, Kenny with a phone in hand. Rebecca couldn't hear who he called, but his response assured her it was someone from an ambulance.

"Get up to the Community Center, now!" He was yelling into the phone, very uncharacteristic for him under any circumstances. "9-1-1 would have taken longer to get to you. Are you coming yet?"

Rebecca was starting to lose her breath, yet another sign she needed to be more active.

Once they had reached the stairs leading into the building, he turned around to wave behind him, signaling to the ambulance driver where he was. "Come in the front." He kept the phone to his ear. "Morey, do you know why he collapsed?"

"No, I found him in the bathroom. He'd been in there a while, and I was heading back down to Kelley Park. I was knocking, and he didn't answer, so I finally went in."

They reached the bathroom in question, and Barry was lying on the floor. Kenny put his phone on the edge of the sink and checked Barry's head but appeared to have found nothing that signified any damage. "Does he have any allergies? Seizures? History of heart attacks? Anything that would cause him to fall down and be unresponsive?" He directed the questions to Morey then spoke directly to the phone while both women watched on from the bathroom doorway. "Male, about seventy, unresponsive on the bathroom floor. Doesn't seem to have hit his head. No pulse." Kenny opened Barry's mouth. "No evidence of obstruction in the patient's mouth."

A loud bang came from the direction of the front doors announcing the arrival of the EMTs.

"Kenny, they're here," Rebecca called out, knowing he'd need to vacate the single-stall bathroom to allow them space to work on Barry. As he exited, he asked Morey the same questions again.

"Nothing. He's never had any major issues."

"Minor ones?"

Morey thought. "Broken bone in high school and he's had the flu a few times, and not even the man-flu. He's really very healthy."

"Rebecca, would you be willing to walk Morey around so we can work?" Kenny tried to give her a look, and she got it.

"Yes, Morey, let's go back outside where we can sit on the steps. They need some space to do their job."

Morey took one more look at Barry lying on the floor of the Community Center bathroom where two EMTs had started chest compressions. It was apparently the first time she had looked because she began to sob immediately. Rebecca wrapped her body around Morey's back using her right arm and took Morey's left elbow in the palm of her hand to escort her to the front. They opened the door and walked out sideways to sit on the front steps.

Knowing they were now out of earshot of the EMTs and Kenny, Rebecca spoke freely. "I know that the people in there will do everything in their power to help Barry. He's an upstanding member of the community and a good person. If he can be saved, they will be the people to do it."

A second ambulance pulled into the driveway with two additional EMTs running past them.

"In the bathroom, main floor," was all Rebecca got out before they were inside with the door slamming shut behind them.

"Can't be good they need more people," Morey said, looking over her shoulder at the closed door.

"Can't hurt."

17

Rebecca had been on the scene too many times to count just now, but she knew when things didn't look good. Barry had been gone from the table too long before Kenny got to him, and Kenny hadn't even started CPR when the EMTs arrived because he was still assessing the body. If Rebecca was already thinking about Barry as 'the body', things were taking a bad turn.

Suddenly, Rebecca stood up and ran inside, returning moments later with Kenny.

"Kenny's going to sit with you for a bit. I'll be right back."

Rebecca took off as fast as her legs and flip flops would safely carry her. She got to the bottom of the driveway and ran across the one-way street before looking for oncoming cars. She had a destination in mind, but she didn't know what she would find when she got there. Reaching the table they had been sitting at for dinner, she took in a long breath, bent over with her hands on her knees and exhaled.

Chapter 3

The Wife

Rebecca examined the picnic table they had been sitting at. She silently thanked some higher power for leaving their discarded plates and utensils right where they had been when everyone left. She realized she had her cell phone in her back pocket and took pictures of the table and dishes before asking for help from a frequent library patron who was eating at the next table over.

"Would you mind watching this table and making sure no one moves or throws away anything. I just need to run over to the table there and get a bag." Rebecca pointed at the tents where people were still turning in tickets for their lobster and chicken dinners.

"Sure. Everything okay, Rebecca?"

"No, but I'm working on it." Rebecca felt comfortable enough to hustle over to the food tent, but she wasn't about to dilly dally.

"Jeremy, can I get one of those empty bags the plates come in? Actually, can I get two?" She realized it appeared she was cutting in line. She turned to the person now behind her and said, "Sorry, just forgot something. I promise I'm not cutting."

"What's going on?" Jeremy's eyebrows drew together, accentuating the wrinkles from years of teaching, as he walked over to the end of the table. Rebecca followed him outside of the line. "I don't like the way you... look."

"I'll try not to take that personally. I'll explain later." He handed the two clear bags over the display of cutlery. "Thanks."

Her trip back to the table was swift. She used a napkin she had grabbed off the table when Jeremy gave her the bags to move Barry's dishes and utensils into them. Once safely inside the bags, she thanked the library patron and high tailed it back up the hill to the Community Center.

As she approached, the EMTs were putting Barry in the back of one of the ambulances. She didn't think she had been gone long enough for them to have already pronounced him dead, but if she didn't believe her eyes, her ears were certainly relaying the same message.

Morey Bornne was sobbing and nearly screaming on the front porch in Kenny's arms. "Why? What happened? Why Barry? Why?"

Rebecca could feel her heart breaking for Morey. It was just this past Christmas someone had died at the Community Center, and that person wasn't very close to her at all. This might have been the end of Morey working in this building.

"Kenny, I need you to take these and maybe find a

fridge for them. I'll stay with Morey." She handed the two bags to Kenny and immediately took Morey into her embrace. "I'm here for you. I'll stay as long as you need me."

Kenny disappeared through the front doors while Rebecca got Morey to sit on the steps. Together, they watched the ambulance drive off, carrying Barry to the medical examiner.

"I just don't understand." Rebecca resisted the urge to respond as if she had been asked a question. She hadn't. Morey was processing, and if she did ask a question, Rebecca was ready for it. "Barry had been eating better and taking his vitamins and medication. He was getting out and walking, regularly." She nodded at Rebecca, letting her know it was the truth. "I just don't understand. Do you have any idea what could have happened?"

Rebecca was asked a question. The answer wouldn't make Morey feel any better, but she could answer it. "We had dinner with Barry. He and Kenny were talking about the softball game and their respective records."

"Barry's was better." She laughed a bit before starting to cry again.

"It certainly was. Kenny told him about the game. Part way through, Barry got up to excuse himself. Said he needed the bathroom. It seemed strange, uncharacteristic, for Barry to get up so suddenly. We commented that it was almost rude how he interrupted and left when there had been several chances for him to leave previously. Mind you, we don't think Barry is rude, just that

21

interaction was off. He was gone long enough for us to finish our meals before you came running down asking for help."

The two women sat together, both considering what Rebecca had said.

"I just can't help but think he'd still be alive if I hadn't asked him to work the dinner." Morey shook her head and dropped it into her hands, her elbows supported by her knees as she sat on the top step.

"Why did you need him to work the dinner?"

"I had some calls from volunteers who had committed but cancelled at the last minute."

Rebecca recalled her chat with Jeremy. "Same reason you called Jeremy?"

"Yes. Now I'll always wonder if I'm the reason Barry is gone." She sat back up.

Rebecca didn't have a good response. Unless Kenny or a medical examiner was able to determine the reason Barry was dead, Morey would always wonder.

"Kenny is amazing at investigating. I'm sure the team we have here will do everything they can..."

"I know, and you said it before. You're right, and I need to let them do their jobs. I can't bring Barry back, and neither can any of you. I expect you'll be helping."

"I'd like to think I already am."

Morey turned to look at Rebecca. "Why? Because you're babysitting me? Keeping me out of their way?"

"No, because when I went back down to Kelley Park, I grabbed the dishes Barry had been using. If there was anything the medical examiner was going to need to know about what he had eaten, I wanted them to have all the possible evidence."

Morey wrapped her arms around Rebecca's neck before Rebecca could brace herself. "Thank you. I can't believe Chief Towne hasn't hired you to be part of the department yet."

"He's asked, and I've turned the job down. I'm more than happy to help without the pressure."

"We're a very lucky town to have the partnership you two bring to the table."

The doors behind them opened loudly, and Kenny exited. "I've put the evidence in the fridge in the basement, Morey. I'll have someone come collect it as soon as possible."

"Of course. Anything else you need?"

Kenny joined them on the top step. "Can I ask you a few questions?"

"Yes. Anything."

"Did you see Barry when he got up here, before he entered the bathroom?"

"I never saw him, only heard. When the door opened, I hollered out to see who was there. He responded that it was him, and by the time I got out of the office, I saw the bathroom door close. That was our entire interaction before I found him on the floor several minutes later."

Kenny took too long to ask his next question, so Rebecca stepped in. "You said he'd been walking and eating better. You also mentioned taking his medication. What medication was that?"

"Blood pressure medication. Started taking it at the

start of the year but had been really on top of it in the past few months. He'd set a reminder on his phone and had one of those pill containers with the days of the week. It was refreshing not having to constantly ask or hound him about taking it." She bent down in front of Rebecca and talked behind her hand as if there was someone nearby she didn't want to hear what she was about to say. "I still checked the bottle to see if the pill count was going down, and I checked the pill box at the end of the night before going to bed, but I didn't have to confront him about it. I really felt like we were gaining years together, him being in better health."

Kenny asked, "Had he been sick lately?"

"I just said he'd been in good health."

"I mean, did he have any minor symptoms of a cold, anything where he'd have taken additional medication that could have interacted with the blood pressure meds?"

She looked deep in thought. "Nothing comes to mind."

"The medical examiner may want to know incase anything other than the blood pressure medication turns up in his system."

"I'm sorry I can't help more. He was in the best shape he's been in for at least the past decade. This shouldn't have happened." She started to cry again.

"Want me to call someone to drive you home? Do you have someone you can stay with?" Rebecca inquired.

"I can drive myself home, but thank you for the offer.

I just need to get my bag with my keys." She stood to reenter the building.

"Morey," Kenny started, "if you could tell me where they are, I'll get the bag and keys for you. I'll also personally guarantee the building gets locked up if you'll leave those keys with me."

"Are you saying I can't go back inside?"

"I'm not saying you can't, but it's probably best if you don't."

She considered his words. "The bag is hanging on the back of my office chair. The keys are inside the bag, and I'll take off the ones you'll need when you bring the bag back."

Kenny opened the door, but it appeared like he was trying to block her from seeing inside. He returned quickly, with the bag, still shielding the inside from view as he carefully slid through the smallest possible opening in the doorframe.

"Here you go. Now, are you sure you can drive home?" asked Kenny.

Rebecca added, "I'll drive your car if you want and have Kenny follow us to bring me back."

"I appreciate the thought, but I'm going to need to do this on my own."

After removing the necessary keys from her key ring and handing them to Kenny, Morey walked down the steps of the Community Center, then down the additional set that stopped at the driveway. She shouted up, "Will someone come out to move the second ambulance so I can get my car out from the back?"

"I'm right on that," Kenny responded, running back in again, this time flinging the door wide. Rebecca made a note to ask about the door once Morey was gone.

An EMT returned before Kenny to move the ambulance and parked it on the road, just across the street from the Community Center, returning to the building as Morey was pulling out.

It took a few minutes for Kenny to come back out, but Rebecca was ready for him. "Why did you prevent her from going back in or seeing inside the building?"

"Honestly, I don't want her to think about it as a crime scene. Santa's Village was one thing, but this was her husband. The fewer memories she has of him dying here, the better."

She looked at him skeptically. "Are you sure that's all it was?"

"Absolutely. I have nothing to hide from you. It's an active crime scene, since we don't know how he died, but I'm not worried about you seeing in there. And, what's with the bags of dishes you had me put in the fridge?"

"When I ran back down to Kelley Park, I found all of our dishes still on the table. I didn't know what happened to Barry, so I packaged his plates up inside bags, without touching them, and brought them up to you. If it turns out to be poison, you'll have something to test. If not, maybe prints? Maybe I'm just overthinking things, but it seemed better to save them than let them get thrown away and regret it later."

Kenny smiled proudly. "I hadn't thought about the food or the dishes. You have a remarkable mind, Rebecca

Ramsey. Whether they become important is yet to be seen, but Morey would thank you for being a forward-thinker if she knew."

"She does know. I told her. I'd rather she wasn't surprised by anything if it's not necessary to keep it a secret from her." Rebecca also wanted Kenny to know everything and not be surprised unnecessarily.

"Remember, we can't pretend that Morey isn't a person of interest if his death is ruled a homicide." He gave her a knowing look. "If the plates do become important evidence, however, I'll make sure everyone at the department knows to give you credit. More importantly, I want my officers to take a page out of your book. Maybe someday you'll write a book about all the crimes you've been a part of solving."

Chapter 4

The Suspects

"Me? Write my own book? I don't think so. I hear patrons in the library talking about the books they have read, and I'm not sure I could take the criticism."

The pair started to walk in the direction of Kelley Park. "I think you'd surprise yourself. You surprise me nearly every day." They shared a look.

Rebecca noticed they had started walking away from the Community Center. "Why are we walking? Don't you need to get back in there for, I don't know, the scene of the death or whatever you call it."

"Jacob is in there, and I need to be down at the park to investigate what happened before Barry died. We both know he was not well when he left the table, and I'd like to see if anyone else felt the same."

"Can I participate?" she asked with a glint in her eye.

"I need this to be official, so you can happen to hear what I'm asking, but that's the best I can offer."

"Offer accepted."

When they approached the line of tents, most of the volunteers were starting to pick up.

Rebecca hustled over to Jeremy before Kenny got to the table. "Jeremy, is anyone talking about anything...unusual?"

"Does this have anything to do with the bags you asked for?"

Kenny stepped up to the table and blocked Rebecca. "Jeremy, do you mind if I ask you a few questions?"

"Sure, Chief Towne. What's this about?" Jeremy stopped boxing up the remaining paper goods.

"Did you notice anything 'off' about Barry when you were working with him?"

"Off? What do you mean? Barry and I were both a little put out that we were working the event, if that's what you mean."

"I mean was he acting the way you'd typically expect him to be? Anything about his speech or mannerisms out of character?" Kenny was having a hard time putting words to the question without leading Jeremy to a specific answer.

"I'm sorry, Chief, but nothing comes to mind. We didn't really have much time to chat with the line being so busy."

"That's fine. Just wanted to check."

Jeremy looked a little sheepish. "Chief, any reason you're asking these questions?"

"If I'm asking, I'm guessing you have an idea." Jeremy responded with a slow nod. "Now, who else was working the line?"

Jeremy responded, "Scotty from the Rotary Club was serving the chicken, April was handing out corn, Kirkland was in charge of the baked potatoes and potato salad, and I was the ticket guy, paper goods guy, whatever needed to be done guy. Barry was, of course, on lobster and butter duty. I think Morey had been on strawberry shortcake, but I'm not positive. Oh yeah, Melinda was handing out drinks. I think that's all of us. The dinner's done in under three hours, so it's not like we really needed breaks or anything."

Kenny had taken out his phone and was using the stylus to take notes. "But who brought you the food? Where was it being prepared? When Barry ran out of lobsters, who got more for him to hand out?"

"Morey would know. I didn't have anything to do with that part."

"I'll see if I can ask around so I don't have to bother her more than necessary, but thanks. You've been a big help."

Kenny looked beside him to Rebecca who had been listening to the whole exchange. Her eyes connected with his, and she motioned an imaginary zipper closing her lips shut.

"Perfect. Let's go see who hasn't left yet."

They walked down the table to find people had already scattered. Rebecca noticed one woman at the very end of the table stacking cans and bottles into crates and assumed it was the person Jeremy identified as Melinda, though she didn't know her. Having just promised not to talk, she waited to see what Kenny did.

"Excuse me, ma'am. Are you Melinda?"

"I am. Who are you?"

Kenny looked down at his outfit. A wrinkled t-shirt and cargo shorts didn't scream that he was the chief of police, so he figured in introduction was warranted.

"I'm Chief Towne. I'm asking some questions about Barry Bornne and wondered if you had any interaction with him today."

"Can I ask why?" Her attitude was difficult for Rebecca to read. Melinda didn't have any reason to expect a stranger would show up asking questions, but she also didn't have any reason to be hostile, did she?

"I'm in the early stages of an investigation, and I was hoping you'd be able to tell me if you worked with Barry at all during the dinner." Rebecca could tell his patience was already running thin.

"I was way down here at the end of the table. He was in the middle. I don't think we said two words to each other. Does that help?" She didn't stop packing up the drinks, her medium-length brown hair covering her face every time she bent over.

"It helps the first part of my question."

This time, she stopped when she stood up straight. "Could you please ask the final part? I'm exhausted, I've been up for like twenty hours, and I'd like to go to bed."

"Ma'am, I'm not trying to bother you, but if you'd rather do this at the station, we have a shiny new room just waiting to be used."

"Please, ask your questions so I can go home."

He took a deep, cleansing breath like Rebecca had

been working on with him. "How do you know Barry, other than working at today's event?"

"I really don't. I grew up around here, so of course I knew Morey, but didn't really have any contact with Barry. I've been in England for several years and just came back only to be asked by my friend April to volunteer here tonight. I'm still jet lagged and need sleep."

"Thank you for your time." He took out a business card and handed it to her. If you think of anything about tonight that stands out as suspicious or you remember anything about Barry, please give me a call. That's my number at the shiny new station."

"Will do. Have a nice night, officer."

Rebecca couldn't hold back, though she'd done a great job so far. "It's *Chief* Towne."

He grinned at Melinda before turning away and heading back down the table to the woman identified as her friend, April, with Rebecca right behind him. April was often on the volunteering circuit in town because she owned a small business, April's Ceramics & Gifts. Volunteering and getting your name out was just smart business.

"April, I'm Chief Towne."

"Your daughters have been in my shop plenty. I know who you are, Chief Towne. Who doesn't?" Her long, blonde ponytail swished side to side as she moved.

"Apparently, your friend Melinda. Not sure she should have been volunteering right after flying back from England."

"She's fine. We haven't seen each other in forever. I'd

already agreed to the dinner before I knew she was coming back this weekend, so I invited her to join me so we'd be able to see each other."

Under her breath, Rebecca said, "Not sure Melinda knew what she was signing up for."

Kenny kicked the side of her foot. "That detail aside, I was wondering if I could ask you a few questions."

"Ask away." April had been moving corn to a clear container from the serving platter when they got to her, but she stopped to focus on them. "Hey, Rebecca."

Rebecca raised her hand but didn't speak.

"April, did you interact with Barry Bornne tonight?"

"How could I not? He's such a card, telling jokes and entertaining everyone in line. I've known Mr. Bornne since I was a kid. Kinda weird to think of him as Barry, even as an adult." It was clear she was familiar with what would be typical behavior for him.

"Was he acting pretty normal for Barry, tonight? Anything uncharacteristic?"

"Just like every memory I've ever had. Why?"

Kenny hadn't revealed to anyone why he was asking questions about Barry, but it would come out sooner or later. However, he waited.

"Just trying to answer some unknowns about a situation, that's all. Thanks for your help, April. If you think of anything else, give a call at the station, won't you?"

"What kind of thing would I call about?" She furrowed her brow and cocked her head to the side, making her look even younger.

"Oh, if you remembered anyone saying anything out

of the ordinary or anything Barry might have done that made you question if he was feeling okay."

She pursed her lips then said, "I will if I think of anything, but he was the same man tonight I've known all my life."

"Well, thank you for your help."

Kenny and Rebecca walked back to the end of the table where Jeremy had finished packing up the paper goods and was now transporting them to the back of a truck.

"Jeremy," Kenny called. Jeremey ran right over. "Have you seen Scotty or Kirkland?"

He pointed to the path, across the playground, that led back up to the one-way street. "I see Scotty heading out, but you'll have to hurry to catch him."

"Thanks." Without waiting, he took off at a run, but Rebecca stayed with Jeremy.

"Are you going to tell me what's going on, or do I have to find out in the paper two days from now?"

"Why do you think Kenny is asking people about Barry?" She returned his question with a question of her own.

At a whisper he asked, "Did something happen to Barry?" She nodded slowly. "Is he dead?" She nodded slowly again. "Ahhhh, crap. Morey must be devastated."

"She is, and she's been sent home. We have no idea what happened. Barry was eating with us, presumably because the line had slowed down enough you could manage without him."

"Yea, Morey came and told him to leave and that

Scotty could hand out the chicken and the lobsters because it was slow. I scooped some butter too, but it was manageable."

"I'm guessing Scotty will be telling Kenny the same thing. If that's the case, Barry was fine before he sat down with us, but not too long into eating dinner, he got weird. I don't know how else to describe it. He excused himself from the table but in a rude way, interrupting Kenny when it was Barry who wanted to have the conversation about the softball game in the first place. It just didn't make sense."

"So, what happened?" Jeremy hadn't gone back to packing up, now fully invested in what was going on.

"He said he needed the bathroom and took off for the Community Center. After a bit, Morey came running down, screaming for help. It was a sad sight when we got up there and Barry was laying on the floor of the bathroom. It just feels like there's no evidence to go on, other than a gut feeling."

"Well, Rebecca, your gut certainly has been helping Chief Towne solve murders around here for over a year now. I'd listen to it."

"I did. That's why I came and asked you for the bags. I came back down and bagged up Barry's plates."

"That seems to be an unlikely source or there would be hundreds of people sick down here from eating the same things, or things cooked together. The corn was all boiled together, the chicken was cooked together, the potato salad was all one big batch, and the lobsters were all steamed in the same pot. The only individual things were the drinks and the baked potatoes."

"Well, I guess that gives me somewhere to start while Kenny is talking to Scotty. Who baked the potatoes?"

"Morey." Jeremy tossed his hands in the air. "She hand wrapped each potato then baked them in the basement kitchen. Granted, someone had to cart them down here for warming, but you're dealing with mariticide if you think she did it."

"That does seem highly unlikely, and we've already talked to the bright and cheerful Melinda who had the drinks. That leaves us with tracking down Kirkland who was handing out the baked potatoes and potato salad."

At the same time, they noticed Kenny was heading back in their direction.

"Quick, talk about something else."

Jeremy obliged. "So, the new box of books came in yesterday, and I've already got them entered in the computer."

"Very funny, you two. I don't believe it for a second. Rebecca, who are we talking to next?"

Chapter 5

The Newcomer

Rebecca looked at Jeremy, knowing they had been discovered. "If we go down the table, we have Jeremy taking care of paper goods and taking tickets. Barry was first with the lobster, then Scotty with the chicken."

"After Scotty was April with the corn and Kirkland with the potato choice," added Kenny.

"Right, then Melinda with the drinks. You've talked to Jeremy, Melinda. Scotty and April. Barry is the deceased, and we still need to talk to Kirkland." Rebecca was checking everything off mentally because she didn't feel comfortable taking notes in front of Kenny. "Obviously, you'll be talking to Morey at another time."

"Let's go see if we can find Kirkland. We should also talk to the people doing the cooking, because they were transferring food to the table all night as well and would have had contact with Barry."

Rebecca didn't move. She was processing how much

larger their list was and how little time they had. "Let's go to where they cooked the chicken and lobsters first. It'll be harder to track them down after tonight."

Kenny nodded. "Sounds like a plan. G'night Jeremy." They walked away from the tents and over to a new area about one hundred feet from where Melinda had handed out the drinks. There were two men and one woman packaging up chicken and lobsters in white, Styrofoam boxes. Kenny got distracted by a local resident who had a question, so Rebecca scooted ahead to the familiar female face behind the table.

"Hey, Reese. Did you handle the chicken or the lobsters tonight?"

Reese looked up. "When the two of you come around, I worry that I'm about to get someone arrested." She continued to close up boxes. "I was cooking chicken. Not about to leave that to the men." Her sassy attitude was exactly the same outside of her restaurant as it was behind her own grill.

Rebecca snickered. "What's the real reason?"

"I'd rather smell like chicken at the end of the night, and there's a lot less heavy lifting."

"Smart woman. Hey, were you the one carting food back and forth to the table for Kirkland to serve?"

Reese shook her head. "Carter and I were responsible for cooking and putting food in trays, and Mungo was walking the trays back and forth."

"Mungo?" Rebecca leaned over the table with the chicken boxes. "Who is Mungo, and how have I never heard that name before?"

"I think it's a nickname, at least I hope it is, and he's newer to the area. Military Veteran and highly service oriented. I've seen him volunteering at a couple things already this summer."

"Good to know. Well, I'm sure Kenny will want to talk to him."

"Rebecca, what's going on? Clearly, you're investigating something. Please tell me I didn't just get someone arrested."

"Of course not. But you did give me some leading information on someone we want to talk to, not a person of interest. We don't even know what we have here."

"Tell me it's a stolen purse or a missing pet. No, never mind, stolen purse." Reese had stopped boxing at this point.

Rebecca whispered, "Barry Bornne died up at the Community Center. We have no idea if it was a heart attack or something completely accidental, but we're covering all our bases before everyone disperses for the night."

"Not Morey's husband. No. Come on. Why'd it have to be him? He was in such good shape, for him, I mean."

"That's what Morey told us."

Kenny approached the table. "Sorry, got sidetracked. Good evening, Reese."

"Evening, Chief Towne. What can I do for you?"

"I'm sure Rebecca already started, but I was wondering if you had any interaction with Barry this evening."

"She hadn't asked anything about Barry, but I'm sorry

to report that I have been standing here for over three hours and have not spoken to Barry. Best I can say is that I saw he was working under the tents. Maybe Mungo spoke with him."

"Mungo?" Kenny asked.

"He's new to the area and likes to volunteer," Rebecca reported.

"Where can I find Mungo?" Kenny asked looking back and forth between Rebecca and Reese.

"Hey, Mungo," shouted Reese. "Chief of Police wants to meet you."

The man identified by Reese as Mungo trotted over to the table, a full head of tight dirty blonde curls bouncing against the top of his ears. When he reached Kenny, he stuck out his hand.

"Chief Towne. I've heard wonderful things about you."

With a wide grin, he replied, "Well, thanks. But I'm sorry to say I've never heard of you until tonight. What brought you to the Newfound area?"

"Luck, I guess. I found a job working up in Plymouth, but the only rental I could find was in Bridgewater, so I took it. I felt like I was drawn more to Bristol and Newfound Lake than Plymouth anyway, so I'm putting down roots in the area, hoping to make it permanent."

"And do you do volunteer work everywhere you live?"

"First place I've lived since leaving the military. Wouldn't mind a little more nightlife, but I'm sure I'll find my people sooner or later. For now, I'm volunteering when I can to get the lay of the land. What can I do for you, Chief?

"I was wondering if you had much contact tonight with Barry Bornne. He was the one..." Kenny was cut off by an overzealous Mungo.

"I know Barry. I've met Morey too. Barry's a great guy. I brought him lobster all night. What about Barry?"

"Had you met Barry before tonight?"

"Uh, yeah. Met him and Morey when I signed up to ump baseball games, why?" Mungo lost the peppy charm he had been riding since getting over to talk to Kenny.

"I was just wondering if he seemed off at any point. Did he change moods or seem unwell in any way?" Again, Kenny was careful not to lead the conversation in any particular direction.

"Nope. We were slinging jokes and one-liners all night. Made the time pass quicker."

"Thanks for that. If I need to catch up with you again, how can I get ahold of you?"

Mungo perked back up. "Working evenings as a host at The Steadfast. Wednesday through Sunday. If it's days, I'm in Plymouth working for CASA. Gotta pay the bills, and trying to put money away to stop renting and start putting down those roots."

"Very admirable of you working for CASA." Kenny jotted down notes. Rebecca assumed they were the locations and dates Mungo worked. "Great to get someone new in town working hard like you. I'm sure I'll see you around at other events this fall."

"You sure will. Nice talking to you, Chief Towne."

Mungo jogged back to whatever he had been doing before Reese had called him over.

"Wow. What a great guy. Seems almost too good to be true," Rebecca remarked.

"Sorry, but you're stuck with me." Kenny lifted her hand and kissed the engagement ring on her finger.

"Not like that. I mean, he's a Veteran and does volunteer work and seems like a great addition to the community. He'll probably be devastated when he learns about Barry."

Reese butted in. "I don't think they were close, but yeah, he'll be upset. Why didn't you tell him?"

"What do you know?" Kenny asked, turning to glare at Rebecca.

"She didn't tell me much, but I wanted to know I wasn't getting someone in trouble. The other one you wanted to talk to was Carter. I can see he's on his way back now. He was cooking the lobsters."

"Was he here with you the whole three hours as well?" asked Kenny.

"Sure was. This is the first time he's left, so I'm guessing it was a bathroom break."

Carter started to slow down as he approached the lobster station. "Everything okay, Reese?"

Kenny responded for her. "Carter, I'm Chief Towne." He extended an arm to shake hands. He returned the gesture, timidly. "I was wondering if you had any interaction with Barry Bornne tonight?"

"Can't say that I did. Reese and I were out straight since before the dinner opened. Now, we've got to box up the leftovers and hopefully sell them to people who are still here."

Rebecca responded quickly, "I'll take four lobsters."

"What are we going to do with four lobsters that are already cooked?"

"I'm going to bring them home and turn two of them into lobster rolls and two will become lobster chowder."

Kenny looked back to Carter. "Four lobsters it is." He boxed four of them, handing them over to Rebecca.

"You'll just need to pay Jeremy back at the start of the table, over there." He started to identify where Jeremy was by pointing.

Rebecca tried to save him some time. "No problem. We know Jeremy."

"Was there anything else you needed, Chief Towne?" Carter asked.

"I don't think so. What's your last name so I can contact you if I need to?" Kenny took out his phone again.

"Cash. Carter Cash." He read his phone number so Kenny could record it. Without having had any contact with Barry, he was probably not going to be asked any follow-up questions.

Rebecca picked up her lobsters and said goodbye to Reese, knowing she could find her again easily if she thought of anything else. She walked away from Carter and Reese with Kenny following.

"I know we just ate, but I need to get these home to harvest the meat and boil the shells."

Kenny scrunched his nose at her. "Boil the shells? Why?"

"To make a lobster stock for the chowder. How else am I going to get lobster stock?"

"Of course you need to boil the shells. What was I thinking?" He was joking now. "I'm going to go meet up with Jacob at the Community Center.

Rebecca stopped in front of Kenny, unable to grab his arm because of her four lobsters. "What about Kirkland? We never talked to him?"

"Scotty said he had already left for the night. I'll need to catch up with him later, but it seems like everyone is agreeing that Barry was perfectly fine until after we sat with him. I don't expect anything different from Kirkland, but I'll still check with him."

"So, I'll see you later?"

"Might be too late, so don't wait up for me. Just not sure what the night will hold." He kissed her cheek then her forehead. "I love you."

"I love you too."

Kenny had started to jog up to the Community Center when she remembered her car was at the library. This wouldn't be a terribly long walk because she could cut through the parking lot of one of the buildings across the street from the library, but with an armload of lobsters, she'd be happy when the walk was over.

After acknowledging a few people on her way through the park, she passed through the adjacent parking lot and crossed the street to arrive at her waiting car. The day had been incredibly long, and a lot had happened. Getting back to her house, seeing her kitties and working in her quiet kitchen barefoot were all so close now.

She entered her home and was immediately jumped on by Bean and Joey, two of the best black cats ever. They attempted to climb her legs while stretching all at the same time.

"Did anyone miss me?" They made a variety of noises, all of which Rebecca interpreted as requests for food.

She dropped the containers on the kitchen counter and immediately fed them wet food and changed their water out. The happy eating noises made her happy.

"While the two of you eat, I'm going to get these lobsters going."

She opened the boxes and started removing meat from the claws, knuckles, legs and tail, leaving no piece of the shell unexplored. When all four lobsters were done, she put the meat in a container bound for the fridge and took out a large cutting board. With all the shells on the board, she wrapped her hand in a towel and broke them all up, cracking the shells as much as possible. Stubborn pieces of claw and knuckle that wouldn't break, got extra attention from her marble rolling pin.

After some additional ingredients and a little time at the stove, she added water and white wine to the shells for them to simmer for an hour or so. While she waited, she went to the living room for snuggle time with Bean and Joey.

"I'm thinking a little *What About Bob?* tonight. What

do you think?" Joey and Bean responded by jumping up on the couch with Rebecca who was unprepared for the company so quickly. "Woah, let me get ready." Before setting her phone on the table next to her, she grabbed the remote and a blanket. "I'll just set an alarm." The alarm was to make sure she didn't leave the lobster stock on the stovetop too long, and she needed it.

Waking up to the alarm, not even having started the movie starring Bill Murray and set on Lake Winnipesaukee, she jumped up to take the lobster stock off the heat and drained it with a fine mesh sieve. Since it needed to cool, she left the lid off and put it in the fridge, perfectly fine with the smell of lobster in her house.

Rebecca, still groggy from her unintended nap, went upstairs, rinsed off and crawled into bed, ready to get the rest of a good night's sleep.

Chapter 6

The Twist

Rebecca woke to the sound of her front door closing and the bed shaking as two cats leapt from their sleeping spots. She was startled but kept her wits about her, checking the time on her phone.

"Three? How is it three in the morning?"

She realized quickly that a door shutting downstairs did not guarantee it was Kenny. She swung her legs from the bed and silently padded across the bedroom, checking for signs it was him from the top of the stairs.

"Bean, what are you doing up at this time of the morning? Hey, Joey."

It was clearly Kenny's voice, so she made her way down the stairs.

"That's quite the wake-up alarm. Nearly scared me to death when I figured out what was going on." She eyed him from head to toe from the second step. "Why are you still in your uniform at this time, and when did you change into it?" Rebecca's head was clear enough to

47

notice he wasn't wearing the clothes from after the game anymore.

"We had a second death tonight. I changed before I responded to the call. Thought about going home after, but, honestly, I didn't want to be alone. I'm sorry I woke you. The door kinda got stuck on the mat, and I didn't want the cats to get out."

"Another one? Who? Are they connected? How..."

"Rebecca," Kenny soothed. "We don't know most of that yet, but it was a man who had recently moved to Bristol. I wouldn't assume you've met him. His name is Ernie. Lives on Union Street. Neighbors called in a noise complaint because his dog was outside barking for hours." Kenny was removing his uniform shirt and pants and folding them neatly in a pile on the floor. "When we got there, a car was in the driveway, but no one answered. We made a forced entry based on the neighbor's statement that he had returned home earlier. When we got in, we found him deceased on the kitchen floor."

"Any sign of a struggle or how he died?"

"Nothing. He'd been dead for a bit, though. Body stiff, even in this heat. No way of telling what happened until the medical examiner gets us more information."

Rebecca hugged Kenny, using the stairs to even their height. "I'm so sorry you've been dealing with this. I know I couldn't, but I wish I could have been there to support you."

"You're right. There's nothing you could have done, but I appreciate the thought. Now, I'm going to tell you something, as long as you don't go jumping to conclusions or harassing the volunteers tomorrow."

She may have thought about crossing her fingers behind her back but refrained. If she broke her promise to her fiancée, she'd have to deal with the consequences. "I promise, no harassing."

"We have reason to believe he was at the Lobster & Chicken Dinner because he had one of the takeout boxes like the ones you got lobsters in."

"But why would he have a takeout box if he attended? What was in the box?"

"From a quick glance, it appeared he had the chicken. The box was in the trash and empty, but the remnants inside the box implied chicken not lobster."

"What about sides?" Rebecca's thoughts were zooming around her brain like the ball in a pinball machine."

"What about the sides?"

"Well, if he was at the dinner, he'd only bring the chicken home that was leftover and probably no sides, right. Or, he may have been late and bought just chicken like the way I bought just the extra lobsters."

"And if I tell you it appeared there had been sides in the box, what would you say then?" Kenny backed away from the shoulders up and looked at her skeptically while still holding her around the waist.

"*If* the box showed signs of potato, corn or another food other than just chicken, I'd say someone bought him a whole dinner and delivered it because he couldn't make it."

"Interesting observation. Our plan was to track down the volunteers we spoke to tonight and show them his picture, see if there was anything worth mentioning about him."

"Like you did for Barry?"

He nodded. "Similar, but we don't think he'd be well known, so more just to confirm he had been there."

"I'm guessing he wasn't. I think you'd be better off asking those same people if they remember anyone picking up to-go orders. That list will probably be pretty short and memorable."

"Why memorable?"

Rebecca started talking with her hands, so he dropped his arms from her waist. "Very few people will have come through asking for a box, right? When you're standing in line, you tend to make small talk, either with the people directly in front of or behind you, and someone is likely to have asked why or who they are getting a box for. People don't generally like silence."

He lifted a hand as if he was going to speak, but she started back up again.

"Also, they'd have to ask for a box. At the very least, Jeremy might have remembered how many boxes he gave out. Maybe he had to go somewhere else to get one. Maybe he was the one to ask why they needed it. I don't know."

"You sure have some ideas, though. Good ideas." He pecked a kiss on her nose. "I'd like to shower and get a couple hours of sleep before I begin a new line of questioning."

"Of course. I'm sorry." She stepped out of his way, and he ascended the stairs. "Want me to make you something to eat or drink?"

"I want you to go back to sleep, and I'll meet you there. I've had enough coffee to keep me awake, but a place to lie down is all I'll need to pass out. See you in the... when we wake up."

Rebecca watched him enter the bathroom and crawled into bed with no intention of going back to sleep. When the shower shut off, she closed her eyes so he'd think she was sleeping, wanting him to feel like he could also go straight to sleep. He did exactly that after exiting the bathroom and didn't wake until eight. Rebecca, however, stayed awake for the next few hours, running scenarios and questions over and over in her head.

First, she wondered if the Lobster & Chicken Dinner had nothing to do with it. This could be a case of two people dying on the same night under completely unrelated circumstances. Second, she wondered if this was two people eating something that was undercooked or tainted in some way. Last, she considered the fact that this could be two connected and purposeful murders. Though the least likely, it was also the sequence of events that could use her help.

When Kenny woke, Rebecca was already in the kitchen making breakfast after having cleaned the whole room an hour earlier. She stood at the stove, taking out a tray of puffed pastry triangles.

"Good morning, sleepy head. I hope I didn't wake you with any banging around. The cooking sheets got stuck together and made quite a racket." They kissed on his way to the fridge.

"Can I get you a glass of orange juice?" he asked.

"A mug, please. I don't like coffee or tea, but drinking out of a mug in the morning feels right. Maybe I'm less likely to drop it because of the handle."

Kenny opened the mug cabinet and selected one from the front. Rebecca had a lot of mugs to choose from because they were her favorite souvenir when she visited new places, not that she had traveled much in the past five or so years.

"Two mugs of OJ, coming right up. What did you make?" He sniffed the air and craned his neck over her shoulder. "Looks and smells delicious."

"I'm not sure that they have an official name, but they are puffed pastry with cream cheese and jelly. I already made a vanilla glaze for the drizzle, though I could be convinced to make the lemon one if you asked nicely." Rebecca smiled back at him.

"Well, given that I have the rest of my life to spend with you, I'll take the lemon glaze next time."

She plated the triangular pastries on two plates, giving each of them a raspberry-filled and a strawberry-filled version. She used a spoon to drizzle the glaze over the top, but not too much. Kenny placed two mugs of orange juice on the kitchen island in front of the stools and took a seat.

"Just because I'm curious, do you not like apple juice? I feel like I should know these kind of things about my future wife."

Rebecca placed the two plates with the mugs and sat next to Kenny. "I'd drink it if it were served to me and I was trying to be polite. I don't hate it, but I wouldn't choose it."

"Are there other juices you'd pick over apple juice?"

"I really only like orange juice, and even then, I'm kinda picky. As a kid, I remember those cans of frozen juice that went in a pitcher with water that got all mixed up. I think they'd probably call it fruit drink or fruit-flavored drink. I can't stand that kind. My preference is fresh squeezed orange juice, but a good bottled version is usually fine. I'm not one to drink something if I don't like it."

"Makes sense. I'm not too picky. I like grape, grape-fruit, cranberry, orange, apple and pineapple."

Rebecca giggled. "Mental note that juice is a safe drink for you. I bet you loved continental breakfasts as a kid. Those places always had a drink machine with strange choices."

Kenny had used his fork to section off a bite of one pastry and stopped on the way to his mouth. "They were the best. I'd get a little of each in my glass. Drove my parents nuts." He ate the bite and his smile widened. "Delicious. You never cease to amaze me."

"You'll have to try both flavors and give me your top choice." Rebecca started to eat her strawberry one first because she like to save her favorite, raspberry, for last.

"Will do."

They shared a quiet breakfast, though Rebecca was biding her time for a few pressing questions.

"I'll have to go into work even though it's a Sunday. Lots of people to question again, and I can't do it over the phone since I need to show them a picture of Ernie since he's not well known."

"Any plan of attack?" She hoped that was subtle enough.

"It's Sunday morning still, so I'll probably wait until after noon. I don't want to impose or show up while people are at church.

Internally, Rebecca did a happy dance. If she knew he wasn't going to interview anyone until after noon, she'd have a little time to possibly get a jump on his investigation. "Makes sense," she said in a disinterested voice.

"I'll head home and change into a clean uniform before I go into the station."

"You shouldn't be headed out in your underwear." Rebecca stopped eating and started to get up.

"I'll put something more appropriate on once we've finished breakfast. I'd hate to get an emergency call in my boxers and undershirt." They laughed together and finished their pastry and juice.

"Well, I wish we'd get a bit more time together today, but I understand. I have so many fun things planned. The litter box needs to be cleaned as does the bathroom upstairs. I have laundry to do, and probably some grocery shopping for the week."

"And you'll never convince me with that lame attempt at diversion that you aren't going to do something associated with this investigation. Please, don't get into trouble..."

"You can't get me out of. I know."

He was ready to leave the house five minutes later, having thrown on a pair of sweats and a hoodie. It was still summer, but the morning was cool enough to pull this off.

"Remember, don't get into trouble," he warned.

"You either." She closed the front door as he got into his SUV, dropped food into the cat bowls, and ran upstairs to take the fastest shower on record.

Chapter 7

The Visits

EVERYONE IN TOWN KNEW KIRKLAND. IT WAS HIS last name, but it often came up first when someone needed help getting things done in town. Last year, Kirkland had been in charge of the Rotary's Penny Sale, but he had stepped away from the Rotary Club to focus on his position as Selectman in addition to being a lawyer. As it was a Sunday, Rebecca knew he'd be at church, so she headed to the foot of the lake to see if she happened to bump into him when he left.

As luck, or good planning, would have it, he stepped out of the church at the end of the service, and Rebecca stepped behind him, hoping to blend in with everyone else leaving.

"Excuse me, Kirkland, might I have a moment?" she asked after tapping his elbow.

"Rebecca Ramsey? What brings you to church? I don't recall ever seeing you here before." He turned and waved to someone else. "See you later, Jane. Good to see you."

When his attention returned to Rebecca, she said, "Well, I had a friend in town for Old Home Day, and they wanted to attend. Who am I to say no to a good service? It was lovely."

He spoke slowly and purposefully. "We were blessed with flawless weather this weekend. Is your friend still here?" Rebecca was mesmerized by his perfectly straight, white teeth that it took her a moment to register and answer the question.

"Unfortunately, no. They had to leave right away, and I stuck around because I was hoping to ask you a question or two."

"Anything for a member of the community." He had a sincere way about him, even if the jawline and cheekbones said Hollywood movie star. He gave her his full attention.

"You left the dinner last night early, so I didn't get to speak with you then. I want to apologize first for bothering you after church."

"No bother at all." He looked at his watch. "I am expected at a brunch soon, though."

"Of course. Did you notice anything last night off about Barry Bornne? Mannerisms, speech, general demeanor?"

"Same old Barry we all know and love. Nothing seemed off, why? Is he okay?"

Rebecca knew she couldn't answer that question

directly. "It was just that he had been sitting with me once he was done serving, and he left abruptly. It seemed out of character for him, and I was worried I had said or done something. I haven't spoken to him since." It wasn't technically a lie.

"I had no issues during service. He was jovial and pleasant. When Morey started to thin out the workers, Barry came through with his lobster, picked up potato salad and corn from me, and went on his way."

"Why did he pick up both the potato salad and corn from you. Wasn't there someone else for the corn? April, right?"

"Yes, but when things slowed down, Scotty started serving both chicken and lobsters, I took over the corn from April, and I think the woman with drinks and Jeremy stayed in their positions."

Rebecca found it odd he didn't know Melinda's name. "The woman with the drinks was Melinda. Did you not meet her?"

"We never exchanged names, if that's what you mean. She didn't give off a particularly friendly vibe. Why?"

"No reason. You just seem to know everyone."

For the most part, the parking lot of the church seemed to have cleared out because cars were not lined up to pull out onto West Shore Road anymore. Rebecca tried to think if there was anything else she needed to ask, because this was probably going to be her only shot.

"Anything else seem out of place or off last night?" A vague, open-ended question was the best she could come up with.

"Did you say that woman's name was Melinda? I've never seen her volunteer before. It's usually the same rotation of community members at those events. That's the only thing that stood out to me."

"You mean like Barry, April, Scotty and Jeremy?"

"Exactly."

"My understanding is that she's a friend of April and that's how she ended up at the dinner. Also, she was jet-lagged from flying in from England."

Kirkland gently put his hands in the air then back down. "That explains it. Always a reason if one is willing to be patient and let themselves be guided to the answer. I do have to be going. Don't want to miss brunch." He rubbed his abs.

"Oh, final thing. Do you know someone new in town named Ernie?" Rebecca struggled to remember details from earlier. "I think he lives on Union Street."

"Can't say that I do. Should I?"

"Probably not. Thanks for humoring me. Have a great day."

"Have a blessed day." He turned and walked away, rounding the bushes at the corner of the church.

Rebecca confirmed that Barry was still in good spirits even when he was finished and picking up his meal, so that wasn't actually helpful at all. She and Kenny thought everything was okay when he arrived at their table, so the shift seemed to happen while they were sitting with him, and even then, it could have just been that he didn't feel well and needed to leave abruptly.

She walked slowly to her car, not wanting to interact with Kirkland again. He waved as he drove past her.

She didn't think she'd be able to do anything with relation to the new person, Ernie, but she could check in again with people from the dinner to see if anyone else knew about him. She knew her time was limited. Checking her phone, she realized it was closing in on noon. If she was lucky, she'd be able to talk to one more person before Kenny started making his way around town.

The idiom *kill two birds with one stone* seemed both appropriate and in bad taste, but if she could find April and Melinda together, she'd get more information in a single visit. April's Ceramics & Gifts was officially closed on Sunday, but she did open for private parties occasionally. Rebecca was going to cross her fingers this was one of those days.

When she pulled into a parking space in front of the ceramic shop, the closed sign was showing but a group of women were having a grand time inside. Rebecca approached the front door and was met by April who unlocked and opened it.

"Hey, Rebecca. I'm not open today. This is a bachelorette party. Did you need something?"

"Any idea what time it'll end so I could come back and chat?" She risked Kenny getting to her first, but time was fleeting.

"I'm guessing we'll be done by one. If we're early, I'll wait for you. Sound good?"

She exhaled. "Sounds amazing. I'll see you then."

Rebecca returned to her car but felt good about the possibility of talking to April again, and maybe even before Kenny. If she was running a party, chances were good that she wouldn't answer her cell or work phone in the middle.

The car was still cool from running the air conditioning between the foot of the lake and the center of Bristol, so she didn't turn it on right away. She did, however, pick up her phone to call Jeremy. Out of everyone at the dinner, Jeremy was the only one with a familiar phone number.

She waited impatiently as it rang. When his voice ended up being a recording to leave a message after, she nearly chucked the phone at the windshield. She hung up and dialed again. After three rings, he answered for real.

"Hello." He was breathing heavily and loudly.

"Jeremy, are you running?"

"That I am, but you called twice, so I figured it must be important. September is just around the corner, and I'm going to be ready for the marathon this year."

"You were ready last year. Why stress about it?"

"I'd like to qualify for Boston, not just do well for my age group. Now, what do you want? Talking and running after fifteen miles isn't as easy as I make it look."

"I was wondering if you remember anyone coming through the line last night and getting their dinner to go in a box instead of on a plate." Rebecca listened to his breathing, waiting for an answer.

"I had a couple requests for boxes because people

didn't finish, but I can't remember anyone coming through and getting the food directly in a box. Why?"

"Before I answer the why, let me ask another question. Have you met someone named Ernie who recently moved to the area?"

"Know anything else about him?"

"He lives on Union Street."

"Do you know anything else useful about him, to help narrow down when or where I might have met this new person in town?" Rebecca could hear cars passing Jeremy over the phone.

"Are you running somewhere safe? I feel like the cars are too close."

"Rebecca. Useful information. Narrow down. I'm quite literally running a marathon right now. No, West Shore Road isn't the safest place to run, so I'd like to keep my wits about me."

She needed to be more efficient. "Nothing else useful. He did have a takeout box from the dinner when Kenny found him in his apartment dead last night, so I'm trying to track down any connection to that box since two people who ate food from the dinner died in the last twenty-four hours."

"Geeze, Rebecca. I'm sorry." It sounded like he had stopped running. "I really don't remember anyone coming through the line asking for a box. The volunteers cooking had the boxes at their station, and I only ran over to get them a couple times after people already went through the line. I wish I could be more help."

"Well, I'm sure Kenny will be asking the same questions later today. I'm just trying to figure out if there's any connection between Barry and Ernie."

Jeremy was still gasping slightly. "Can you ask Kenny for more information about Ernie? Is he also looking for connections?"

"It was three in the morning when he got home, and I didn't get to ask much of anything. I wasn't there, so he really shouldn't tell me, and I know better than to push my luck."

"Well, if you come up with any other details about Ernie, or any other questions, feel free to call me back. However, I may wait to return the call until after I have showered."

"Fair enough."

Rebecca panicked. "Don't hang up. I forgot to ask if you got dinner last night. I heard Barry and April got excused early when the line started to die down, no pun intended, and they got a free dinner. Did you?"

"I did. Chicken, of course, for the protein. Why is that so important?"

"Two people died either during or after eating at the dinner. One had lobster and the other chicken. I was thinking, maybe something happened at the end of the dinner that didn't impact people who went through the line earlier. I don't know, just a hunch."

"I may have been one of the last people to take food. I ate it in the park, on a plate, and I was and am fine. Keep looking though. The connection you're hoping for is probably just around the corner. Now, if you would be so kind as to let me finish this self-inflicted torture I call a hobby, I can go home and complain to my dinner of salmon, beans and avocado that I'm sore and tired."

"I'm so sorry I can't join you for that experience. Thanks for your help."

"Sorry I couldn't do more. Later." He disconnected the call.

Rebecca stared at the front of the ceramic shop, deciding to turn on the air conditioning. If Kenny was going to show up and spoil her chance to talk to April first, the least he could do is let her join him.

Chapter 8

The Friends

Rebecca watched as the party involved, what she felt was, a lot of drinking and not much crafting. She had nothing against alcohol, but this particular group of women seemed to be making up for everything Rebecca *hadn't* consumed since turning twenty-one.

Eventually, women started to hug and disperse, heading out of the front door in singles and pairs, waving as they walked by the glass storefront to their cars. The last person to leave was, surprisingly, Melinda. Rebecca jumped out of the car and quietly approached Melinda as she walked away from the ceramic shop.

"Melinda? Is that you?"

The woman who had been extra cranky at the dinner last night turned and smiled at Rebecca while still walking, only slower.

Recognition crossed her face in a flash causing her to slow further and walk backward until Rebecca was at her side. "Oh, I owe you an apology. I was so tired from traveling and then having to volunteer, I'm sure I was much shorter with you last night than I should have been. Can you forgive me?"

"Already done. You had every reason to be tired, and we can't always control how it'll all play out when exhaustion kicks in."

"I'm glad we ran into each other again." Melinda continued walking, presumably back to her car or wherever she was staying.

"You were at the bachelorette party," Rebecca stated. "Who's getting married?"

"April, actually. She wanted to get all her friends from high school and college together before the big day next weekend. By getting here yesterday, I was able to see so many people who came for the Lobster & Chicken Dinner and the party today. Now, I'll have five days to visit family and places I haven't been to in years before the wedding Saturday and a flight back to England on Sunday."

Rebecca was intrigued. "You must have been very close to fly back for a whole week for her wedding. Are you a bridesmaid?"

"Maid of Honor, actually. April put her own shower together because I couldn't get back early enough to do it. Just affording the flight and dress was a stretch."

"Who are you staying with, if you don't mind me asking?"

Melinda laughed. "If you can believe it, I'm staying with her parents. They still live up on Church Street, same house as when April and I were kids having pillow fights in elementary school. I'm staying in the spare room." Rebecca could see from the far off look on Melinda's face, she was imagining them back then.

"That's wonderful. Where's the wedding? I'm still in the planning stages of mine and can't commit to the location."

"Once Inn a Lifetime. She got so lucky. There was a cancellation, and she was on a list of brides with flexible dates. Obviously, we're thrilled for her."

Rebecca remembered the last time she was at Once Inn a Lifetime for a wedding, one she'd never forget. While she was sure April's would be perfect, it wasn't on her list of potential wedding locations.

"She's very lucky to have someone so supportive, such a long-term friend."

"Thanks for saying that, but it's what anyone should do for their best friend, even if we haven't seen each other for four years."

"Four years." Rebecca couldn't hide the surprise in her voice. Showing up like that after four years was rare. "What have you been doing in England?"

"Took a job out of college with a satellite office in London. Nothing was holding me here, so I went. I'm enjoying the ease of traveling around Europe and meeting lots of people. Travel while your young, they say. Whoever *they* is, was right."

Rebecca was enjoying their chat but decided to return to the original purpose of stalking the ceramic shop. "I did have another question from last night, if you don't mind."

"What was that about, anyway? You and a police officer were asking odd questions."

"Chief Towne is my fiancée, and we had a situation pop up during the dinner, and I thought of something after everyone left." Rebecca shifted her weight from one foot to the other. "Did you notice anyone going through the line with a takeout box? You know, picking up a dinner to take with them instead of eating at the park?"

"I didn't really notice since I was at the end with the drinks, but they did give those of us leaving at the end Styrofoam containers for our dinners. When April was allowed to leave, she went through the line with a plate and later transferred everything to a box and waited for me. When I went through, I just used the box to package up the free dinner I earned volunteering."

"So you think others who stayed late got to take theirs in boxes as well?" This was news. Jeremy reported that he couldn't remember seeing boxes going through, but he got a plate and ate there. The volunteers with boxes must have been going through later than he did.

"Several at the very end. We got to take extra too, if we wanted it."

Rebecca was thinking of the people who could have provided a boxed dinner to Ernie, and the list just got longer. She hoped to still talk to April before Kenny, and then give him a call with this possible development he might not already know about.

"Well, I'll cross my fingers that everything goes well this week and with the wedding. Maybe you'll find a reason to return to the states sooner than four years this time."

"Maybe. April hopes to have children right away, so I'd definitely have to return for that."

"Feel free to stop in at the library. I'll be there all week." Rebecca realized when she invited Melinda to visit that if she didn't get to everyone today, it would be difficult to work around her work schedule starting tomorrow.

"See you around." Melinda continued walking in her original direction.

They hadn't made it far from the front doors of April's Ceramics & Gifts when she started the conversation with Melinda, so backtracking would be quick. Occasionally during the conversation, Rebecca had looked over her shoulder to check for Kenny, but he hadn't shown up. Maybe luck was in her corner.

The bell of the front door chimed as she entered, checking around for April.

"I'm back here. We're closed today," reported a voice from a back room.

"It's Rebecca. I came back to chat."

"Can you flip the lock on the front door?" said the voice.

Rebecca turned around and rotated a metal knob, securing the front door from unexpected visitors.

April entered the main business space at top speed, clearly still cleaning up from her own party. "Lots to do, and so little time."

"I'll help. I'm here bothering you on a day you're

closed and, from what I hear, celebrating your upcoming wedding. Congratulations."

"Thank you. Thank you." April beamed at the mention of the wedding.

"And I hear you managed to get a spot at Once Inn a Lifetime. You must be beside yourself."

She let out a sigh of relief. "I had settled on a location, but I really wanted the beach at Once Inn a Lifetime for as long as I could remember with the reception in the barn. One of my proms was in that barn."

"One of mine too, but several years earlier." She coughed at the word several. April was maybe in her late twenties, so there was quite a gap between the two proms they were talking about.

"I know from the talk about town that you and Kenny are engaged and still haven't set a date or location. What's that about?"

Rebecca was too stunned to speak. She knew that they tried, in the beginning, to keep their relationship quiet or at least not flaunt it, but thinking that people in town were talking about their wedding plans, or lack thereof, was unsettling.

"I... We... The wedding details haven't been finalized, but we're working on them."

April seemed to have realized the subject was delicate and responded with, "It will all work out exactly as it should." She placed a gentle hand on Rebecca's shoulder. "Now, what did you want to talk about?"

Shaking off the funk from moments ago, Rebecca remembered why she was there. "I just talked to

Melinda, and she said people were given takeout boxes at the end of the night last night if they volunteered right to the end, but you had a plate. Is that accurate?"

"Rebecca, where is this going? Plate? Takeout box?" April started cleaning again, looking up occasionally.

"Look, something pretty significant happened yesterday that I'm not allowed to discuss, but I'm just trying to nail down some details that may or may not be important, and a takeout box just might matter. What I'm really trying to do is figure out how many possible diners left with a takeout box." She hoped she hadn't gone too far.

"Well, I don't remember seeing any go through the line, only plates. I noticed Reese had some over by where they were cooking the chicken and lobsters, so I got one and transferred mine. Does that help?"

"Somewhat. I was given one when I bought extra lobsters at the end of the night, but not a full meal. I also know where my takeout box is, so I'm not that concerned about it."

"I wasn't hungry at the end of the night and wanted to bring mine to my fiancée. He works hard and has a long commute, that's why I took it in a box."

That was something Rebecca would have done for Kenny if he had to work. "What does your fiancée do for work? Do I know him?"

"Probably not. He works about an hour south. We can't wait to move in together after the wedding. The long-distance relationship thing has been hard. We met three summers ago when I visited the coast. At the time, he was a part-time lifeguard on the weekend, and I was trying to get noticed on the beach. I gave him my number, and he texted me that night for a date. The rest, as they say, is history."

"So, it's been long-distance since then?"

"I've always lived with my parents. My mother has some disabilities, so I care for her with my father. I could never move away where I couldn't continue to help, so I set up my ceramic shop here in town. Any man I fell in love with would need to accept my family situation, not just me."

"And you think you found him?"

"Absolutely. He finally moved into the area where we'll start our married life together next weekend."

The hairs on the back of Rebecca's neck stood on end, a cold sweat gathering at her hairline. The next question she asked would irrevocably change April's future.

"April, what's your fiancée's name?"

"Ernie, why?"

Rebecca paused. She knew what she knew wasn't sharable, but now she'd need to talk to Kenny sooner than ever. "Just wondered if I'd met him. You said he's new to the area? I haven't recently met anyone named Ernie."

"I'll be Mrs. Ernest Budding by this time next weekend."

Rebecca wasn't about to pop that bubble. Letting her know the truth was way above her pay grade, but connecting the dots for the investigation was something she was happy to help with. "And I'm sure you'll look beautiful. I'm going to get going." She hooked a thumb over her shoulder as if she was practicing her hitchhiking moves.

"Good to see you again so soon. Have a nice day."

April didn't know just how bad her day was about to get, and Rebecca felt like it was all her fault. "See you later."

Rebecca flicked the lock open so she could exit. When her feet hit the sidewalk, her face ran into the chest of her own fiancée.

"Why am I not surprised to see you here?"

She hooked her arm under his elbow and started to shuffle him away from the door. "You can't go in there yet."

Chapter 9

The Stages

"I know you like to think you're part of this investigation, but you can't tell me what to do. I was exceptionally foolish telling you my plan today."

"No, I just saved you from shoving your foot in your mouth. You've got very limited time to figure out what you're going to say to April."

Kenny balked. "Why do I need to figure out anything?"

"Because she just told me that Ernie, a guy who just moved to town, into the apartment they are about to share, is her fiancée, and their wedding is next weekend. She's here today because she just had the bachelorette party for a wedding that's never going to happen."

"What?"

"Yeah. You're welcome. I just saved you from finding out like I did. Now, what are you going to say to her?"

"I don't know what to say. Are you sure?"

Rebecca rolled her eyes. "I mean I didn't ask if the

apartment was on Union Street, but I'm sure you can confirm that and his last name before you tell her that her soon-to-be husband was found dead on the floor of their soon-to-be apartment last night. Had you not figured out any next of kin for him yet?"

"We've got a vague time of death and a last name now, so I can go in and ask some questions to confirm that he is her Ernie, but I still haven't told his parents. I mean, they would typically get to know before a fiancée."

"I'd be willing to go in with you, to help soften the blow or just to be a shoulder to cry on for after you tell her." Rebecca felt even worse now that she might have to be part of breaking April's heart. "Let's just go ask a few questions. Maybe she'll tell you who his parents are so you can call them sooner than later."

Rebecca followed Kenny into the shop, the same bell alerting April to their presence. They were lucky she hadn't locked it behind Rebecca. If they had knocked, April probably would have ignored them.

"We're closed," she hollered from the back room.

"April, it's Chief Towne. I wanted to ask you a few questions."

She poked her head out. "Hey. I just... Rebecca, you're still here."

"Just caught Kenny on his way in. Figured I stick around." She felt immeasurable guilt knowing that April would also be angry with her for not telling her what she knew as soon as she put the puzzle pieces together.

"Have you come up with new questions for me,

Chief Towne?" She said his name in a joking way, as if she didn't respect him, though everyone in town did.

"I wanted to know more about your upcoming wedding. Rebecca here just told me this had been a bachelorette party. Do I know the lucky groom?"

"His name is Ernie, and he just moved to town, so probably not. He keeps his nose clean, works hard and only has eyes for me." Her fluttered eyelashes showed just how in love she was.

"What's his last name?"

"Budding, why?"

"Just trying to figure out if I know him. I do know one Ernie, but he's lived in town forever and old enough to be your grandfather, so I'm guessing it's not him."

"Not my Ernie. He's twenty-nine and handsome as can be."

"Do you both have family coming in for the wedding?"

April's sappy, lovesick persona drooped. "Ernie's parents have both passed. He was only seven when he lost his mother, and his father passed last year. He'd been sick a long time. We considered moving up the wedding, but it was Ernie's decision to wait so I could get the location of my dreams. I've lived in Bristol my whole life and always wanted a beach wedding on Newfound."

"April, I'm sorry to have to be the one to tell you this, but I was called for a noise complaint last night on Union Street. A dog was tied up outside, barking incessantly. We had a report from the neighbors that the resident who owned the dog had come home, so we forced entry to do a well-check based on the canine neglect."

"Where are you going with this? My Ernie would never leave Bruno outside like that. It must have been someone else's dog."

"Is Bruno a bloodhound?

"Yes, but..."

Kenny put his hand up, interrupting her protest. "April, when I entered the residence, I found Ernie on the kitchen floor. He was pronounced dead at the scene. I'm so sorry, April. Ernie Budding is dead."

April went through all of the stages of grief in front of them, back to back. "Ernie's not dead. We're getting married next week. He just can't be. I mean, I'd give anything to keep him safe, anything. He can't be dead because I'd protect him at all costs. He's the love of my life."

Rebecca tried to stop the unraveling, but it was already in motion. The gesture to potentially hug April sent her over the edge into uncontrollable sobbing. She dropped to her knees, attempting to catch her breath between wails. Kenny and Rebecca stayed where they were.

"NO!" She finally regained the ability to speak, standing and swiping the newly painted pieces of pottery off the table, smashing them into fragments on the floor. At this point, where her own physical harm was possible, Kenny approached and wrapped her in a bear hug facing away from him. He held her arms down at her sides while she fought to free herself.

"April, I know this is a shock," Rebecca said in a calm voice, "but I'd be willing to call someone to come be with you. Your parents? Melinda?"

She continued to fight for her freedom for several minutes while Kenny and Rebecca patiently waited, speaking silently between each other with their eyes every so often. When her anger seemed to have dissipated, she sagged, letting all of her weight fall into Kenny's arms.

Together, he lowered himself and April to the floor of her ceramic shop, making sure to check for debris before allowing her knees to hit the floor. "April, I know Rebecca offered, but we can contact someone to come be with you or to come pick you up. How can we help?"

"Melinda should be at my parents' house by now, up on Church Street. I don't want to see my parents yet. Can you call and ask for her to come back?"

"One of us can go get her. If I'm not mistaken, she doesn't have a car. It'll take longer if she walks back. Who do you want to stay with you?"

"Rebecca, can you stay?" April looked up at her, all fight gone.

"Of course. Kenny, can you go pick up Melinda? April's parents live on Church Street."

He stood and walked around to the front of April. "I know where your parents live, and I'm more than willing to go get Melinda, if that's who you want."

"Yes, please."

"Do you want me to tell her, or do you want to?"

"You."

Rebecca wrapped her arms around April, both sitting on the floor now. When Kenny left, April looked directly in Rebecca's eyes. "Did you know? When you came in earlier, did you know it was my Ernie that had died?"

"Not until you told me about him, right before I left. I knew someone had been found in an apartment on Union Street, but I had almost no information about him. I didn't even know until you told me this morning when I arrived that you were..."

"Getting married next weekend. That's a phone call I don't want to make. Ugh. That's a lot of phone calls I don't want to make. So much money and time for an event that will never happen. I'll never move out of my parents home. I'll never get to start my adult life. I'm going to be that old lady in town with a little shop that no one knows how it stays open. They'll tell stories about me." April threw her arms up in defeat.

"I'm sure, right now, while this is brand new and raw, it feels that way." Rebecca had been the speech giver many times now, but it never got easier, and there was never a *right* thing to say to someone grieving. "You're young. You still have years and years ahead of you to make whatever choices you want to make. I'm sure when Melinda gets here, she'll help you with all of the details and phone calls that need to be made."

"Who is going to tell my parents?" She started to sob again, dropping her face in her hands. "I'm sure they were also looking forward to getting their house back. My mother couldn't stop telling everyone about this wedding and all the details, bragging to anyone who would stand still what a great man I had found and how she didn't know what he saw in me."

"He saw the love of his life, otherwise he wouldn't have proposed. I'm sure he wouldn't want you to say negative things about yourself on his account."

They sat in silence for several minutes, waiting for Melinda to rejoin them. When Kenny returned, he walked back in the shop behind her.

"April, Chief Towne's just told me what happened?" She dropped to the floor as Rebecca stood, scooping up her life-long friend in a strong embrace. "I don't know how to help, but I'll do whatever you need me to do."

April didn't respond, and Kenny excused himself, motioning for Rebecca to join him outside. When the door had closed behind them, he grabbed her elbow, moving her away from the shop window. Once off to the side, he turned her to face him, both hands firmly on her shoulders.

"Woah, what's up?"

"Last night, when we found the takeout box from the dinner at Ernie's place, I called the medical examiner and asked if they could put Barry and Ernie at the front of the line to test whatever was in their system. I also had Jacob drive the box from Ernie's and the plates you saved from Barry as well to the same office."

"What did they find?"

"Besides the fact that I now owe a very important medical examiner a very large favor I don't want to even imagine, they found no trace of drugs or poison of any kind. She just called me when I pulled up to pick up

Melinda. One man had eaten lobster, while the other had chicken. They both had corn on the cob and potato in their system. However, there was this one extra ingredient that isn't standard at the Lobster & Chicken dinner."

"Are you saying both Barry and Ernie consumed something fatal, and it wasn't poison?"

"I'm saying they both consumed something in the final moments of their lives that shouldn't have been in their system from the dinner."

"Have you found any connection between Barry and Ernie to narrow down a suspect?" Rebecca was practically bouncing. The new information Kenny was currently withholding might be the key to how both men died.

"We have found no connection between the two men other than eating food from the dinner and ingesting the same unexpected ingredient."

"Is it possible that other people have died as well and we just don't know it yet? You know, like how Ernie was found dead in his house hours later."

Kenny inhaled as if he was about to speak then paused for a moment. "I suppose that is possible."

"And did you take into account that Ernie didn't go to the dinner? His takeout box was given to him."

"We've been assuming he picked it up and left with it. Do you have evidence that supports a different narrative?"

"I spoke with April, and she said she wanted to bring her box to her fiancée because she wasn't hungry.

Everyone that worked got a free dinner. Those that stayed late took them home in takeout boxes. Actually, April took hers on a plate and transferred it to a box, but that's how Ernie got his."

"You don't think..."

"I don't know what you're thinking."

Kenny proceeded to gesture for Rebecca to look at his phone. He showed her the extra ingredient in both systems as reported by the medical examiner and confirmed with secondary testing of the two food containers. She grabbed his phone and located an article about poisonous plants and where to find them.

"If this is the ingredient that killed them both," she said, "I'm fairly confident I know who did it, but why?"

Chapter 10

The Finale

Before reentering the ceramic shop, Kenny made a phone call to Kirkland.

"Good Afternoon. I've got a couple questions for you that just can't wait. Do you have a minute?"

Since Kirkland was a Selectman for the Town of Bristol, Kenny had his number saved. The phone call didn't last long, and Rebecca was able to ascertain where he was going with it. The problem was getting April or Melinda to say enough to incriminate the guilty party.

Kenny and Rebecca had a quick meeting of the minds just outside of Melinda and April's view then opened the door once more. It seemed to Rebecca, from a quick glance, that April had stopped crying, only to start again once she saw the duo enter.

Rebecca was the designated person to start the new inquiry based on her support for April immediately after learning the news of her deceased fiancée. Kenny felt it would be too aggressive for him to start.

"April, we had a couple more questions. Just hoping to narrow down if this was an accident or intentional. Would you possibly be able to answer them so Chief Towne can get the investigation started?"

She sniffled and wiped her nose on the sleeve material at her shoulder. "I suppose. Melinda, could you grab a water from the fridge in the back?"

"Of course." She jumped up and dashed to the back, returning quickly with a plastic bottle in her hand. "Need anything else?"

"I don't think so. Go ahead, Chief Towne." April sipped the water.

Kenny cleared his throat. "At the dinner last night, your station for the corn was adjacent to Kirkland who had the potatoes, correct?"

"That's right. He was handing out baked potatoes or potato salad to each paying customer."

"At any point, did you take over for Kirkland or help him out?"

"Nope." She sniffled again. "Neither of us had difficult jobs, and there was no reason for us to leave."

Kenny started to ask a new question, but April picked back up again too quickly.

"Well," she said, turning to Melinda, "there was that one time where you came over to help Kirkland because he was sent to get more baked potatoes, right?"

Kenny and Rebecca shifted their eyes to Melinda. "I did. Since I was the one at the end of the table, one of the cooks hollered to me to get someone to pick up more baked potatoes from them. I didn't think I'd be able to carry that heavy of a tray, so I sent Kirkland, and I took over, also handing out potatoes for a few minutes. I was right next to him, so it was easy to do both the drinks and potatoes as each person came through."

Mentally, Rebecca realized this line of questioning wasn't very helpful, since both women had been on either side of Kirkland and his potatoes. She decided to deviate from their plan of attack.

"April, you also said you brought dinner to Ernie last night."

"That's not exactly what happened."

Kenny took over. "What you've told us is that you bought a dinner and ended up transferring it to a takeout box intended for Ernie because you weren't hungry. What part of that isn't exactly what happened?" Rebecca could tell he was trying to keep the frustration out of his voice, but he wasn't doing a great job of it.

"I got a phone call that my mother needed me. Dad had gone out and wasn't answering his phone, so she needed me to come home immediately. I let Melinda know, since we only had the one car, that I was leaving early and could come back sometime later to pick her up, but she volunteered to bring dinner to Ernie for me. It's not a long walk to Union Street from Kelley Park, and she's such a great friend and maid of honor. I'm so lucky you're here," she said to Melinda. The tears flowed, and Melinda swept April up in her arms.

"Maybe you should come back some other time. Clearly, April needs a break from this line of questioning. This is too much for her," Melinda suggested.

"Actually, the next question goes to you, Melinda. Did you bring a dinner to Ernie?"

"I did."

"Was he there when you delivered it?"

She huffed, holding her sobbing friend. "He wasn't. April knew he'd be home soon, so I left it on the step outside."

"Did you notice if his dog was inside or outside when you visited," Kenny said, tersely.

"The dog wasn't outside, or I wouldn't have left a box of food on the step." She returned her answer in the same clipped tone.

Rebecca's friendly demeanor was justified at this point to bring down the personality conflict brewing between Kenny and Melinda. "Do you remember which box of food you left for Ernie?"

"What do you mean?" asked April, who lifted her head up from Melinda's shoulder.

"April, you had a box of food you had picked up, and Melinda had a box of food she had picked up. Melinda, do you remember which one you delivered to Ernie?"

April looked at her friend. "I didn't even realize you didn't get dinner." Turning to Kenny, she said, "I had mine in my hand when I ran to take care of my mother, not realizing that I should have left it with Melinda. I ended up giving mine to my mother, so you must have given your dinner to Ernie. Again, a better friend than I."

The shop was silent. Kenny looked at Rebecca, Rebecca looked at April and, eventually, April looked at Melinda.

"Why did it get quiet? Don't you have any more questions?" Rebecca and Kenny both acknowledged they heard April by looking at her, but shifted their gaze to Melinda, giving her an opportunity to speak.

"Why are you both looking at me?"

"Melinda, this is your opportunity to answer April, if you'd like to do so before we finish the story of last night."

"Finish the story?" April asked. "If all you want is for someone to finish the story, I can do that. Melinda walked back to my parents' house, we stayed up and watched an old episode of Columbo my mom had started then went to bed. This morning, Melinda came here to help me set up for the bachelorette party, which seems completely pointless now."

"Melinda, is that all April needs to know?"

Melinda looked at April then back to Rebecca and Kenny. "Yes. What else would I need to tell her?"

"I've already spoken to the medical examiner. There were two deaths related to the Lobster & Chicken Dinner, and both victims ingested the same poisonous plant. The ingredient was part of the potato salad. It resembles celery, which is why both victims didn't suspect anything, but it's native to the UK. Melinda, you just returned to Bristol from England, did you not?"

April looked at Melinda, her mouth wide and jaw slack. "Melinda, what did you do?" She scooted back, bumping into one of the crafting tables.

"We're currently in contact with both airports and searching April's parents' home for evidence of you transporting the hemlock water-dropwort under the guise of being celery, maybe pretending it was going to be an in-flight snack. The easier thing, Melinda, would be for you to tell us why you murdered Ernie Budding and Barry Bornne too."

"Murder? You murdered Barry too? What do you mean, too? What is going on here?" April stood up and moved to stand with Rebecca and Kenny.

Melinda stood last. "Barry was an accident. When Kirkland left to get the baked potatoes, I dumped half of what I had into a container of potato salad and mixed it up under the table, intending to take it myself. When Kirkland returned too quickly, I lost track of it. I didn't know who it got handed out to. I'm sorry that someone else was impacted by my carelessness."

"But you're not sorry that my Ernie is dead?"

"Nope."

All three adults standing near the door of the shop were equally stunned into silence.

"I didn't know it would be so easy. The plan was to swap whatever you had with the box I made up, but when your mom needed you at the last second, I didn't even need to swap anything. Poisoning Barry is unfortunate because that's probably what got me caught. No one would have thought Ernie's death was due to celery, or even the Lobster & Chicken Dinner at all. There would have been no medical exam and no investigation. With his parents dead, no one would have pushed further into finding out what happened. It would have been signed off as 'just one of those things,' and I would have been here for emotional support for the week."

April started sobbing all over again and gasped, "Why? What did Ernie ever do to you?"

"What didn't he do? You and I... we were in constant contact. Phone calls, text messages, sending memes at crazy hours of the night because they reminded us of each other. All that stopped when you got serious with Ernie. With a wedding next weekend and a baby on the horizon, I was going to lose my friend forever. I couldn't let that happen, not over some man."

"That man was the love of my life. You could have told me you missed me or that I was distant. I had no idea you felt this way."

Rebecca noted that Melinda seemed completely void of emotion during the whole exchange.

"It wouldn't have worked. This would have, if I hadn't made a mistake. One simple error, and I messed it all up."

"Do you really think *that* was the mistake, losing the first dish of potato salad? Melinda, the first mistake was thinking you had the right to control my life like that, my future. I never want to see you again."

At that admission, Melinda let a single tear fall. "Guess you're going to arrest me," she said, directed at Kenny.

"We are." He picked up his radio and asked for Jacob to enter, which he did. "Jacob, please read Melinda her rights and take her to the station. She has confessed to killing both Barry Bornne and Ernie Budding."

"Sure thing, Chief." Jacob walked around the unmoving group of April, Rebecca and Kenny. He took handcuffs out, put them on Melinda's outstretched wrists and escorted her to a waiting cruiser.

Once they were gone, Rebecca turned to April and grasped her hands. "I can't believe I'm going to say this, but when we found out how Ernie was poisoned, I was so worried you were involved. I just didn't see a way for it to not have been you. I'm so glad that we came into this situation with an open mind and let her say enough to confess."

"I'm thankful that you did, but whatever would make you think I was involved?"

"I didn't know about you getting taken away from the dinner to care for your mother, so I assumed that you did take your dinner to Ernie like you said. I was devastated thinking you had or were capable of killing someone. After the last year or so, I've learned that nothing is ever what it seems."

Kenny's radio began to squawk. "Chief, we found more of that plant up here at the house on Church Street."

"My parents' house? Where?"

Kenny pressed the button to respond. "Where did you find it?"

"In a container in the fridge. Not much left, but we think it's a match. We'll bring it in."

"Be careful," Kenny responded. "Now, April, can I drive you home to be with your parents?"

"I was on the lease for the apartment with Ernie. Can I go there, or is it still a crime scene?"

Kenny thought for a moment. "I don't see why you

can't go there. We don't need to do anything else. Do you need a ride?"

She started picking up the shop. "No. I'll take my time here and drive over when I'm ready. Thank you, Chief Towne, Rebecca. I'm not sure this would have come to light without the two of you. The area is very lucky to have a team like you."

"Just part of the job." Kenny nodded and smiled.

April looked over at Rebecca. "What's your excuse?"

"I love a good mystery."

Out on the sidewalk, once it was only Kenny and Rebecca again, they locked eyes.

"So, any chance you'll reconsider and take me up on a job where you work with the department on an as-needed basis?"

"I already do that, and you don't have to pay me. Don't you think the taxpayers prefer the current arrangement? I know I do. I get to paint outside the lines."

"That's what I'm worried about."

Rebecca began to walk to her car. She opened and sat inside just long enough to turn on the air conditioning. When she got out, she asked, "What do you want for dinner?"

"Heather has that date, so the girls will be with me tonight."

"The girls will be with *us* tonight. So, what do *we* want for dinner?"

"I'm going to say that we should order pizza and watch a movie. School starts way too soon, and then everything will be scheduled. I know they're not your favorite, but do you want fried pickles from the pizza place with dinner tonight?"

"Only if I get mushrooms on my pizza. And make sure to order extra pickles if the girls want some. Wouldn't want to share everything." She gave Kenny a big kiss for anyone to see. "Just text me when you three are on your way over. I'll whip up something for dessert. Love you."

He waited for her to sit in the driver's seat and closed the door for her. When she rolled down her window, he said, "I love you too."

PLEASE LEAVE A REVIEW!

★ ★ ★ ★ ★

Virginia K Bennett

An Appetite for Solving Crime

THANK YOU FOR READING MY BOOK!
I WOULD LOVE TO READ YOUR FEEDBACK ON
FACEBOOK, INSTAGRAM, AMAZON, OR
SIMPLY SEND AN EMAIL TO:
authorvirginiakbennett@gmail.com

Recipe

Puffed Pastry Triangles
Ingredients:
1 Sheet of Puffed Pastry
(I prefer Jus-Rol in the refrigerated case)
1 Jar of Jelly/Preserves
1 block of softened Cream Cheese
2 Egg Whites
Coarse Sugar
1/2 Cup Powdered Sugar
1/2 tsp Vanilla
Milk

Thaw puffed pastry according to the package, if frozen.
Cut into 6 squares.
On one half of the square, diagonally, spread cream cheese almost to the edge then add about two tablespoons of jelly/preserves.

Fold the square diagonally and seal the two edges with a
fork.

Brush egg whites on the top of the triangle with a silicone
pastry brush then sprinkle with coarse sugar.

Bake on parchment paper at 425 degrees for about 12-15
minutes.

Makes 6 triangles.

To make the glaze, sift powdered sugar into a small
mixing bowl. Add vanilla. Add 1 Tbsp of milk at a time,
mixing until you get the preferred viscosity. Drizzle over
the triangles.

Also by Virginia K. Bennett

A Newfound Lake Cozy Mystery:

* * *

The Mysteries of Cozy Cove:

Much Ado About Muffin

It's All or Muffin

Muffin to Lose

Nothing Ventured, Muffin Gained

You Ain't Seen Muffin Yet

Here Goes Muffin

* * *

Ice Cream Truck Mysteries:

Chilled to the Bone

About the Author

When she's not writing on her couch with her two cats, Twyla and Geo, Virginia is busy teaching middle school math, grocery shopping, cooking or spending time with her husband and son. Together, her small family loves to go geocaching and visit theme parks.

Mysteries have always been an interesting challenge for Virginia, much like watching a magician perform. Unless you want to hear the entire thought process behind who she thinks is the killer and why, you might want to avoid watching any movies together.

The path to publishing a book is different for everyone and her path is full of twists and turns. Thank you to those who support the journey.

facebook.com/VirginiaKBennett

instagram.com/authorvkbennett

Made in United States
North Haven, CT
23 July 2024

55223165R10059